# CATS
## HIDDEN PICTURES

Selected by Jody Taylor

Boyds Mills Press

**COVER**

**Bike Hike**

Before Kitty rides away, can you help her find the spoon, shovel, shoe, baseball cap, eyeglasses, artist's paintbrush, musical note, pen, carrot, crayon, pencil, and the key?

Copyright © 1995 by Boyds Mills Press
All rights reserved

Published by Bell Books
Boyds Mills Press, Inc.
A Highlights Company
815 Church Street
Honesdale, Pennsylvania 18431
Printed in the United States of America

Publisher Cataloging-in-Publication Data
Main entry under title :
Cats hidden pictures / selected by Jody Taylor.—1st ed.
[32]p. : ill. ;   cm.
Summary : Various objects are hidden in illustrations of cats.
ISBN 1-56397-437-1
1. Picture puzzles—Juvenile literature. [1. Picture puzzles.]
I. Taylor, Jody. II. Title.
793.73—dc20    1995    CIP
Library of Congress Catalog Card Number 94-72628

First edition, 1995
Book designed by Tim Gillner
The text of this book is set in 10-point Clarendon Light.
Distributed by St. Martin's Press

10 9 8 7 6 5 4 3 2 1

**Raining Kittens**

It's raining kittens! But a lot of other things are falling from the sky, too. Can you find the glove, cupcake, sailor's hat, wristwatch, rabbit, butterfly, crown, shark, hammer, handbell, whistle, cup, and the rolling pin?

3

## Treasure Hunt

Mick, Mac, and Marie are searching for buried treasure. While they're looking at the map, you can look for the fish, cup, bird, rabbit's head, bee, snail, paper clip, turtle, apple, acorn, carrot, crab, sewing needle, mouse, and the number **7**.

## Laundry Day

The triplets are helping Mother Cat with the laundry. Before the last towel is hung, see if you can find the lizard, mouse, handbell, key, flashlight, screwdriver, hockey stick, sewing needle, carrot, hunting bow, arrow, book, hammer, parrot, and the accordion fan.

**Gardening Fun**

Greta is planting her garden while the scarecrow looks on. Neither of them sees the twenty-one hidden birds ready to steal the seeds. Can you find them before it's too late?

**Gone Fishing**

The Fur Folks are enjoying a "purrfect" day of fishing, but they're catching more than fish. Can you help them hook a glove, sewing needle, sock, comb, butter knife, fishhook, spoon, rabbit, nail, fork, shark, mallet, and a ring?

**Belling the Cat**

While Master Cat is in dreamland, the mice want to tie a bell around his neck so they'll know when he's nearby. Can they do it before Cat wakes up? Maybe the forty-four mice hidden in this picture can help. How many can you find?

**The Cheshire Cat**

Alice has just met the talking Cheshire cat. As they chat, try to find the stopwatch, book, top hat, key, apple core, teapot, piece of cake, mouse, cup, bottle, crown, rabbit, and the jar.

**Fright Night**

It's nice to have a friend around during a scary movie. Before you get too frightened, try to find the ice-cream cone, trowel, nail, bird, ladder, cat's head, mirror, sheep, pennant, cane, artist's paintbrush, arrow, fish, heart, and the letters **C**, **F**, **L**, and **V**.

11

**Bedtime Story**

It's bedtime, but Mama Cat is the only one who's tired. Maybe you can help quiet the kittens by reading off the hidden objects: eyeglasses, apple, mouse, pencil, fork, light bulb, caterpillar, bell, candy cane, horn, flashlight, two feathers, bird, nail, and the handbell.

**Party's Over**

The birthday party is over, but Shelly and Kelly are just starting to have fun. Can you help them find some things to play with? Look for the arrowhead, fountain pen, crown, snake, ring, strawberry, crescent moon, eagle's head, boomerang, fork, baseball bat, and the man's face.

**The Owl and the Pussy Cat**

It's a lovely evening for a sailing trip. As Owl sings to Pussy Cat, see if you can find the light bulb, sewing needle, mallet, mouse, saltshaker, broom, cup, bird, sea gull, kite, spoon, book, rabbit, and the seashell.

14

## Goblins and Whiskers

These goblins are out for some trick-or-treating fun. They don't see all the things lurking around them. Do you? Try to find the eyeglasses, sewing needle, ladle, pitchfork, spoon, whale, rabbit, scissors, coat hanger, baseball cap, artist's paintbrush, and the hammer.

## Country Ride

Father Cat and the kittens are taking a ride in their new car. They're having so much fun they don't see the toothbrush, book, pizza, hamster's head, rabbit, crescent moon, weasel, spoon, mouse, cardinal's head, hot dog, and the pencil.

**Cooking Secrets**

These cats are cooking up some special treats. Before Lacey tells Alex the secret ingredient, see if you can find the duck, banana, cupcake, trowel, artist's paintbrush, key, crayon, oar, fish, slipper, rabbit, sailboat, ice-cream pop, and the kite.

## Witch's Spell

It's Halloween night, and Winny the Witch's magic spell made nineteen cats disappear into thin air. See if you can find them before the sun comes up.

## Cat Fishing

It looks as if Holly caught her furry friend on the end of the line. Next, she can fish for the shark, bird, trowel, artist's paintbrush, pencil, high-heeled shoe, carrot, snail, hat, fish, dog's head, bell, snake, and the frying pan.

**Dessert Time**

Five hungry kittens are ready for some cake. After they eat they can look for the squirrel, flashlight, spoon, key, slipper, pencil, frog, two mice, fork, handbell, bell, two feathers, bird, and the nail.

**Puss in Boots**

This clever cat can fool the king, but can he fool you? Try to find the pencil, bell, crescent moon, hammer, apple, boomerang, flag, lizard, megaphone, bird, ruler, fish, open book, and the artist's paintbrush.

**Ball of Fun**

When the people are away, the cats find all sorts of fun. They don't even notice the bird, nail, candle, heart, cupcake, ice-cream cone, feather, whistle, crescent moon, flashlight, hard roll, seashell, and the slice of cheese.

**Chasing Butterflies**

Gilly can't quite reach the butterfly, even with Hildy's help. But maybe he can reach the banana, open umbrella, rabbit, arrow, teapot, trowel, bell, duck, wishbone, fish, bee, crescent moon, hummingbird, lion's head, and the bat.

## Best Friends

Sir Cat has decided that making friends with mice is easier than chasing them. Together they can look for the carrot, sailboat, dog, piece of pie, broom, loaf of sliced bread, pencil, toothbrush, lollipop, piece of cake, trowel, pushpin, baseball bat, seal, tube of toothpaste, and the mug.

## Housepainting

If the cats ever finish painting the house, they can look for the cardinal's head, spoon, glove, bird, hammer, butterfly, dog's head, chicken, mouse's head, gopher, pliers, open book, pencil, fish, and the dragonfly.

## Feline Philharmonic

Marley Mouse sneaked inside to enjoy the beautiful music. Before anyone notices her, see if you can find the nutcracker, hamburger, bell, boot, envelope, rabbit's head, fork, lamp, box, camera, house, carrot, cane, snail, tennis ball, and the cracked egg.

**Catnap**

Max is surprised to see a bold mouse curled up with Uma, the Champion Mouse Chaser. As they snooze, try to find the artist's paintbrush, trowel, dragonfly, duck, rooster, sailboat, fishing pole, butterfly, acorn, fish, crescent moon, purse, and the toothbrush.

**The City Mouse and the Country Mouse**

City Mouse is enjoying a delicious treat, but Country Mouse isn't sure the food is worth the risk. Before Cat leaps at a feast of his own, try to find the diamond ring, megaphone, chicken, paper clip, banana, key, fish, pair of pants, comb, coat hanger, eyeglasses, book, eagle's head, and the ladder.

# ANSWERS

**Cover:** spoon, shovel, shoe, baseball cap, eyeglasses, artist's paintbrush, musical note, pen, carrot, crayon, pencil, key

**3:** glove, cupcake, sailor's hat, wristwatch, rabbit, butterfly, crown, shark, hammer, handbell, whistle, cup, rolling pin

**4:** fish, cup, bird, rabbit's head, bee, snail, paper clip, turtle, apple, acorn, carrot, crab, sewing needle, mouse, number **7**

**5:** lizard, mouse, handbell, key, flashlight, screwdriver, hockey stick, sewing needle, carrot, hunting bow, arrow, book, hammer, parrot, accordion fan

**6:** twenty-one birds

**7:** glove, sewing needle, sock, comb, butter knife, fishhook, spoon, rabbit, nail, fork, shark, mallet, ring

**8-9:** forty-four mice

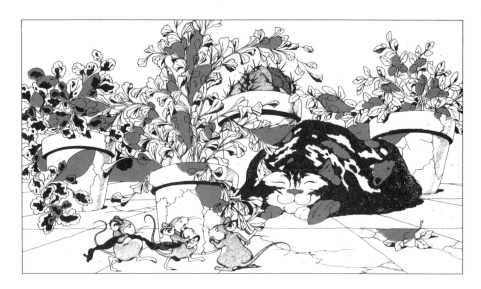

**10:** stopwatch, book, top hat, key, apple core, teapot, piece of cake, mouse, cup, bottle, crown, rabbit, jar

**11:** ice-cream cone, trowel, nail, bird, ladder, cat's head, mirror, sheep, pennant, cane, artist's paintbrush, arrow, fish, heart, letters **C**, **F**, **L**, and **V**

**12:** eyeglasses, apple, mouse, pencil, fork, light bulb, caterpillar, bell, candy cane, horn, flashlight, two feathers, bird, nail, handbell

**13:** arrowhead, fountain pen, crown, snake, ring, strawberry, crescent moon, eagle's head, boomerang, fork, baseball bat, man's face

**14:** light bulb, sewing needle, mallet, mouse, saltshaker, broom, cup, bird, sea gull, kite, spoon, book, rabbit, seashell

**15:** eyeglasses, sewing needle, ladle, pitchfork, spoon, whale, rabbit, scissors, coat hanger, baseball cap, artist's paintbrush, hammer

**16:** toothbrush, book, pizza, hamster's head, rabbit, crescent moon, weasel, spoon, mouse, cardinal's head, hot dog, pencil

**17:** duck, banana, cupcake, trowel, artist's paintbrush, key, crayon, oar, fish, slipper, rabbit, sailboat, ice-cream pop, kite

**18:** nineteen cats

**19:** shark, bird, trowel, artist's paintbrush, pencil, high-heeled shoe, carrot, snail, hat, fish, dog's head, bell, snake, frying pan

**20:** squirrel, flashlight, spoon, key, slipper, pencil, frog, two mice, fork, handbell, bell, two feathers, bird, nail

**21:** pencil, bell, crescent moon, hammer, apple, boomerang, flag, lizard, megaphone, bird, ruler, fish, open book, artist's paintbrush

**22:** bird, nail, candle, heart, cupcake, ice-cream cone, feather, whistle, crescent moon, flashlight, hard roll, seashell, slice of cheese

**23:** banana, open umbrella, rabbit, arrow, teapot, trowel, bell, duck, wishbone, fish, bee, crescent moon, hummingbird, lion's head, bat

**24:** carrot, sailboat, dog, piece of pie, broom, loaf of sliced bread, pencil, toothbrush, lollipop, piece of cake, trowel, pushpin, baseball bat, seal, tube of toothpaste, mug

**25:** cardinal's head, spoon, glove, bird, hammer, butterfly, dog's head, chicken, mouse's head, gopher, pliers, open book, pencil, fish, dragonfly

**26:** nutcracker, hamburger, bell, boot, envelope, rabbit's head, fork, lamp, box, camera, house, carrot, cane, snail, tennis ball, cracked egg

**27:** artist's paintbrush, trowel, dragonfly, duck, rooster, sailboat, fishing pole, butterfly, acorn, fish, crescent moon, purse, toothbrush

**28:** diamond ring, megaphone, chicken, paper clip, banana, key, fish, pair of pants, comb, coat hanger, eyeglasses, book, eagle's head, ladder